Grayson, Avery, and Austin,

Eva and I are <u>so</u> happy
to share our story with you.
We had so much fun working
together. We are sure you will
enjoy being part of the adventure
by doing the activities on
each page.

Have fun!
Love,

Kay Dragen
2022

The Tale of Scout's Unfortunate Tail

An Interactive Story

Sondra Kay Dragoun
illustrated by Eva Ott

Publisher: Book Baby 2022

ISBN: 978-1-66785-757-2

The Tale of Scout's Unfortunate Tail

This is an interactive story, and you are invited to become part of the adventure! "Need some help?" Sooner or later we all need someone there to encourage us when we need a helping hand, to guide us when we are confused or have taken the wrong path, and to celebrate with us no matter how small our victories. The story of Scout and Gypsie tells of two such friends who enjoy just spending time together. As you read the adventure, look for their instructions. Gypsie and Scout will ask you to do something interactive - crow like a rooster, count objects, find something in the pictures. Please answer the question and do the action before you turn the page! Be sure to share the story of Gypsie and Scout with a friend!

Have fun!

To our family, Kary, Bryan, Ivy, and the many friends who inspire us.
To all the animals in the world who have taught us to be kind
and to love one another.

It happened not-so-long ago in a land not-so-far away that there lived a most wondrous dog named Scout. Mighty and proud, he would stalk under the midnight summer stars and protect all of the creatures of his town, Ottsville.

News of his courage and power spread throughout the land, so there was very little to worry about in this quiet kingdom where girls had beautiful names like Ivy and Eva and Kary and Del. Neither creatures nor humans dared to disturb this peace-filled place.

As it would happen, there was one inhabitant, however, who found trouble quite without even looking for it. Just down the road lived Gypsie, a carefree dunderhead of a dog who never looked for trouble but always found mischief. She was a frequent companion of Scout.

Neighbors thought Scout's goodness might rub off; it never did. When a pail of paint was overturned or someone's cucumber patch became a tangled mess, it was usually Gypsie who was blamed. All of this was about to change.

It was one of those evenings when the moon seemed to invite everyone to play outdoors. Gypsie and Scout were lying by the tranquil stream; four front paws dipped lazily into the cool water.

It was a frequent game they played with craw daddies and tadpoles who wagged and tagged the two bank creatures. They all knew it was just a friendly game.

How nice to be at water's edge the whole night with no cares about passing time. Balloon-throated frogs were in chorus with the night wind while fireflies danced just out of reach.

As many times before, our two friends lingered until both heads sank, and soft snores added to the pleasant hum of nature.

"Cook-a-doodle-doo! First light!"
cried a far-off rooster.

"Come. I'll treat you to breakfast," was Gypsie's first comment as she slid into a ground-hugging stretch.

For weeks Gypsie had been passing Farmer Bean's chicken coop and helping herself to one fresh egg - the biggest one she could find. Tired of the intrusion, the angry hens clucked and flapped but to no avail.

Farmer Bean was angry too. He had twelve hens, and he expected twelve eggs!

Who would pay for only eleven? He had customers waiting, but there was never a full dozen. He had to do something!

Farmer Bean had hammered and nailed,
measured and sawed.

Can you find the hammer?

The giant trap was set! Today he would catch
whoever threatened his hens!

Scout had heard stories about how eggs make one's fur shine, and I must admit he was a bit tempted, but he replied, "No, I think I will go home, and I suggest you do the same."

Gypsie tossed her head to the side, thought for a while, then quickly trotted down the trail to the familiar coop.

It was an enormous trap with lots of wood and metal. Gypsie should have smelled it, but her thoughts were filled with the flavor of the egg.

Can you find the egg?

Her nose led her, and so she slowly stepped her paw into the coop the same way she had dipped it into the water.

SNAP! BAM! THUD!

Gypsie was hopelessly trapped!

Worried, Scout had followed Gypsie just out of sight and had watched everything. "'I'll free you this once, but you must promise me you will always think before you act."

Breathlessly, they both pushed and tugged.

Angry hens threw their feathers!

Gypsie and Scout could hear Farmer Bean's shouts growing closer!

With one last trembling heave Scout pushed
the mighty gate up just enough to allow Gypsie
to crawl sideways under it. But the weight of
the great trap was more than either anticipated.

Just as both were about to leap to safety, it fell
right down on the unfortunate tail of Scout!
Both raced away into the woods glad for
their lives.

What is
Farmer Bean
holding?

From that day forward, Gypsie seemed to have new-found wisdom and gained the respect of the entire community because of her careful attitude.

What about our hero Scout?

Though tailless, Scout still guarded the countryside with dignity because he knew what we all know that the length of one's tail has absolutely nothing to do with the measure of one's honor.

Now that you have read our story, would
you like to draw a picture and write more
about Gypsie and Scout?

Share your story
with a friend!

Kay

At an early age my imagination was stoked while riding a tractor on my family's farm. I roamed the pasture chasing insects, following animal tracks, and watching nature change with the seasons. My imagination was my best friend. Field mice, birds, deer - all became characters I wove into endless adventures. Recently I shared a story about the friendship of two dogs with my artist granddaughter and told her, " I think my story has potential. You could make it come alive with your art!" Since then it has been an adventure for the two of us as we exchange our thoughts about words and pictures. We are eager to share our story. Grab a friend and actively participate!

Eva

I have had the passion for art ever since I was little. I enjoy the challenge of trying to captivate emotions with an artwork. When my grandmother came to me with the story for this book, I imagined colorful and playful illustrations for the words. I am so excited for everyone, young and old, to read the tale of Scout and Gypsie!

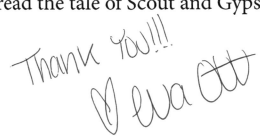

Thank You!!!
♡ Eva Ott